D1505590

FIELD HOCKEY FIRSTS

BY JAKE MADDOX

illustrated by Tuesday Mourning

text by Eric Stevens

Impact Books are published by Stone Arch Books
151 Good Counsel Drive, P.O. Box 669
Mankato, Minnesota 56002
www.stonearchbooks.com

Library of Congress Cataloging-in-Publication Data
Maddox, Jake.
  Field hockey firsts / by Jake Maddox ; text by Eric Stevens ; illustrated
by Tuesday Mourning.
     p. cm.
  ISBN 978-1-4342-1606-9
  [1. Field hockey—Fiction.] I. Stevens, Eric, 1974- II. Mourning,
Tuesday, ill. III. Title.
  PZ7.M25643Fie 2010
  [Fic]—dc22

                           2009004078

Summary:
Fiona's new school doesn't have an ice hockey team, just field hockey!
She decides to try out for field hockey anyway, but the sports have
different rules. Will Fiona be able to stay on the team if she doesn't
learn the rules?

Creative Director: Heather Kindseth
Graphic Designer: Emily Harris

Photo Credits: Shutterstock Images/ Vladimir Korostyshevskiy, cover
(background)

Printed in the United States of America

TABLE OF CONTENTS

. . . .

Chapter 1

MOVING IN

Fiona Roth was sitting on a cardboard box in an empty bedroom in her new apartment. She didn't feel like she was at home, but she was.

All around her were cardboard boxes and big, bulky suitcases. In the corner, posters were rolled up in tubes leaning against the wall.

"Are you unpacking?" her mom called from the other room.

Fiona sighed. She was supposed to be getting her bedroom set up.

"Yes, Mom," she called back. Then she got up and opened the box she'd been sitting on. It was full of her hockey equipment.

"Well," Fiona said to herself, "at least this town has a hockey team."

Fiona loved hockey. She had been one of the best players on her middle school's ice hockey team. And the other players were her best friends. Life was great.

That is, life was great until her mom got a new job and they had to move down to the city.

Fiona had spent her whole life — till now — living in a small town way up north. Everything was different there.

There were lakes everywhere. Houses were sometimes miles apart. Between them were huge fields and forests.

River City was totally different. First of all, the city was much bigger than the town Fiona had lived in.

There were no lakes at all. Plus, almost everyone lived in an apartment, not a house.

The apartment Fiona's mom had found for them was half of the top floor of a big, square building.

There was a back yard, but they had to share it with the people who lived in the other three apartments. And anyway, it was a tiny back yard. Nothing like the woods that were behind their old house.

It was going to be hard to get used to.

One of the last things Fiona had done in her old house was to look online for information about the middle school she'd be going to. She quickly found out that they had a hockey team. Smiling, she had turned off her computer and packed it up with the rest of her things.

Now, in her new bedroom, Fiona reached into the hockey equipment box and pulled out a puck. She tossed it up and caught it.

"My lucky puck," she muttered. Just then, her door opened.

"Fiona," her mom said. She looked disappointed. "You haven't done much unpacking."

Fiona shrugged. "I know," she said. "I will."

Her mother sighed. "I know you're still sad about moving," she said.

Mom walked over to Fiona and took the puck. Then she smiled. "Remember," she said, "tomorrow you can join the hockey team at your new middle school. It's all you talked about on the drive here."

Fiona tried to smile as she reached out and took the puck back. "That's true," she said. "It'll be great to get on the ice."

"Now start unpacking," Mom said. "I'll order us a pizza."

Fiona smiled. "Okay," she said. Then she walked over to another box and started unpacking her clothes.

Chapter 2

HOCKEY WITH A BALL?

Fiona's alarm clock buzzed the next morning at six o'clock. She moaned as she rolled over and smacked the clock.

"Wake up, sunshine!" her mom called from the kitchen. Fiona could hear her mom clanking plates and glasses, setting the table for breakfast.

Fiona didn't feel very sunny. It was her first day at a new middle school, in a new city.

Everything was going to be completely different from her hometown. She was not excited about it at all.

Fiona slowly got dressed. Then she stomped to the kitchen. She shoveled her cereal into her mouth, chewed quietly, and drank her juice. She didn't say anything.

"Healthy breakfast," Mom said. "It's very important."

Fiona grunted her agreement. She chewed the last of her cereal and looked at her mom. "Write me a note," she said suddenly.

"A note?" Mom asked. "For what?"

"Say that I don't have to go to school," Fiona told her.

"Oh, Fiona," Mom replied with a sigh. "Don't start."

Fiona slowly got up from the table. "Fine," she said. "Send me off to misery and sorrow."

"Drama queen," her mom replied with a laugh. "Have a good day!" she added as Fiona left the apartment with her bag.

The new middle school was only a couple of blocks from their apartment. Fiona walked slowly down the sidewalk. She was in no hurry to get to school, after all.

Soon, though, she reached the front of the school building. Quickly, she felt around in her bag for her lucky puck. It was scratched up from too much use on the ice back home, but she loved it.

She gave the puck a quick rub and took a deep breath.

"Here goes," she said. Then she pulled open the door and stepped in.

It was chaos.

There were kids everywhere. Some were gathered at their lockers, shouting about their weekends. Others were in their own world, listening to their MP3 players. Others looked as lost as Fiona felt.

Fiona gripped her puck tighter and walked on.

Mom said to go to the office first, Fiona told herself. She looked ahead and spotted a small sign that read "Office," so she headed that way.

She was about to open the door and walk in when she overheard something.

"I'm so excited for hockey season," someone said.

Fiona stopped and turned. Two girls were sitting on the bench outside the office. One was a bit taller than the other and had very long, dark hair. The other was small with short, mouse-brown hair.

They looked her up and down. For a second, Fiona hoped she was dressed cool enough for her new school. She tried not to worry about it.

"Did you say hockey?" Fiona asked them.

"Yes," said the smaller girl. "Who are you?"

"Oh, I'm new," Fiona replied. "I'm Fiona."

"I'm Aliyah," said the taller girl. "And this is Selma."

The other girl waved.

"Nice to meet you," Fiona said. "I played hockey back home. I mean, my old home. I'm hoping to join the team here, too."

"We're actually waiting here to sign up for tryouts," Selma said.

Fiona beamed. "Oh great!" she exclaimed. She shook her head and said, "I just can't wait to get back on the ice."

Selma and Aliyah glanced at each other.

"Um, the ice?" Aliyah said. "What are you talking about?"

Fiona started blushing. "The ice," she repeated. "You know, as in hockey?"

Selma and Aliyah started laughing.

"What's so funny?" Fiona asked.

"Ice hockey?" Aliyah said through her chuckles. "You play ice hockey?"

Fiona was confused. "Yes," she said. "Don't you?"

Selma shook her head. "We play field hockey, Fiona," she explained. "There is no ice hockey team here."

Fiona was stunned. She'd been looking forward to playing hockey again so much. She hadn't thought about the fact that most schools didn't even have girls' ice hockey teams. Up north, it was so cold that everyone played ice hockey. But in a lot of schools, only the boys played — if anyone did!

Aliyah finally stopped laughing. "It's okay, Fiona," she said. "You should join the field hockey team anyway."

Fiona frowned. "I don't know," she said. "Hockey with a ball?"

The other girls laughed again. "You'll get the hang of it," Selma assured her.

Fiona shrugged. "I guess I might as well," she said.

Aliyah nodded. "Right," she said. "It's not like you can play ice hockey alone anyway."

Chapter 3

BULLY BULLIES

The rest of Fiona's first day at the new middle school went by in a blur. She met her teachers and her classmates. She walked around the school, sometimes lost, looking at a map of the school the principal had given her in the morning.

"I never needed a map at my old school," Fiona muttered as she tried to find her way around after school. "The locker room has to be around here somewhere!"

A girl bumped into her. "Watch it," the girl said.

Fiona looked up and saw two girls glaring at her. "Sorry," Fiona said. "I'm a little lost."

"Look, Jess, she has a map," one of the girls said.

"I know, Paula," said Jess. "She's not used to big buildings. They live in barns where she's from."

Paula laughed. Then the two girls walked away.

"That was rude," Fiona muttered as she walked on.

Finally, she found the locker room. She was a few minutes late already, so she quickly changed and ran out to the field for the hockey tryouts.

Coach Kelly stood in the middle of the field. The team sat in a circle around her.

Before joining the circle, Fiona looked up and down the field. The first thing she noticed was that it was bigger than a hockey rink. It looked more like a soccer field.

There was a center line, and a line on each defensive side, just like in hockey. But the crease — the half circle surrounding each goal — was much, much bigger.

Fiona looked at the circle of girls sitting around the coach. She was happy to see Selma and Aliyah. But then she spotted Jess and Paula, the two girls who had been rude to her in the hall.

"Anything we can do for you?" the coach asked, looking up at Fiona.

"Oh, I'm Fiona Roth," Fiona said. "Sorry I'm late."

"You're the new girl," Coach Kelly said. "That's okay. Take a seat." Fiona smiled and sat down next to Selma.

"Oh, great," Jess said. "Farmer Fiona wants to be on the team." Paula cracked up laughing.

"That's enough, Jess," Coach Kelly said. Then she turned to Fiona. "Fiona, Selma tells me you played ice hockey back home."

"That's right," Fiona said. "I played forward."

"Well, you'll pick this up quick enough, I should think," the coach said. "Just remember: there's no checking in field hockey. I don't want to see anyone get hurt, okay?"

Fiona nodded. "Okay, Coach," she said. "No checking. Got it."

The coach got the girls into two teams for a scrimmage. Fiona was glad when Coach Kelly put her on a team with Selma and Aliyah. She was worried she'd end up with Jess and Paula, who obviously didn't want her around.

The practice game went pretty well at first. Soon, though, play stopped for a penalty call.

"I need a forward from each team," the coach said. She picked up the ball.

Fiona knew from ice hockey that the face-off would come next. That would get the game going again.

"I'll do the face-off, Coach," Fiona called out. She ran over to the coach.

Right away, Jess and Paula started laughing.

"The 'face-off'?" Paula said in a mocking tone. "Coach, seriously! She doesn't even know how to play."

"Okay, Paula," the coach said. "Keep it to yourself."

Then the coach turned to Fiona. "In field hockey, we start play again with a 'bully,'" Coach Kelly explained. "It's a little different from a face-off in ice hockey."

Fiona blushed deeply and stood back. "Oh," she said timidly.

"Just watch for a while, and you'll see what I mean," the coach added.

Selma walked over to the coach to do the bully for their team. Paula did the bully for the other team.

The coach placed the ball on the ground between them. Suddenly, the two girls slapped the ends of their sticks together three times. It made a loud clapping sound.

Then Selma slapped the ball backward to Aliyah, and the game was back on.

"This is not hockey," Fiona muttered to herself.

With a sigh, she tried to keep up with the action. But it was like trying to watch television in a different language. She felt completely lost.

Chapter 4

MORE STUDYING

It was a long week for Fiona. Selma and Aliyah did their best to be nice to her, but it didn't help much. Jess and Paula were still giving her a hard time. Fiona kept going to field hockey practice, but she was sure she wouldn't end up making the team.

On Friday, Coach Kelly posted the names of the girls who had made the field hockey team. Fiona was sure she wouldn't be on the list.

"There is no way I made the team," Fiona said to Aliyah and Selma after school. They were walking fast down the hall toward Coach Kelly's office.

"Sure you will," Aliyah said.

"I don't even know the difference between a field hockey field and a soccer field!" Fiona said nervously. "The sticks look like candy canes to me. How could I make the team?"

"You're a good athlete, that's how," Selma replied. "That's the most important thing. You can learn the sport easily."

"Right," Aliyah agreed. "Besides, it's not that hard to make the team."

The three girls reached Coach Kelly's office and waited for the crowd of girls to clear.

While Fiona waited for a space to look at the list, Jess and Paula stepped out of the crowd.

"You're lucky, farm girl," Jess said. She sneered at Fiona.

"Yeah," Paula added. "You may have made the team, but trust me, you won't like being on the team."

"We're not going to make this easy for you," Jess explained, glaring at Fiona. "You can count on it."

With that, the two mean girls strode off.

Selma and Aliyah looked at their new friend. "Well," Selma said eventually, "at least you made the team, right?"

Aliyah chuckled. Just then, Coach Kelly stepped out of her office.

"Fiona Roth?" the coach said.

"Here, Coach," Fiona replied.

The coach walked over to her. "First of all, good job. You made the team," the coach said.

"I heard," Fiona replied. "Thanks."

The coach nodded. Then she said, "Now, I can see you're a good athlete, but you'll need to study up on the rules of field hockey a bit."

"I know," Fiona said.

The coach pulled a booklet out of her pocket. "Study this," Coach Kelly said. She handed the booklet to Fiona.

"Um, okay," Fiona said. She glanced at the cover of the booklet. It read "Field Hockey – Rules and Regulations."

Coach nodded. Then she went back into her office.

"It's like homework," Fiona said to Selma and Aliyah. "This is so weird. I've been playing hockey since I knew how to walk. I really don't think I need to study."

Fiona flipped through the booklet. "Seriously," she went on. "This is ridiculous. I learned to skate when I was about two. I was holding a hockey stick in no time. And now the coach expects me to study for a hockey team?"

Selma laughed. "Well, it is a little different," she said.

"I have enough studying for math, history, and language arts," Fiona said. "How will I have time to study hockey? This is crazy."

"Don't worry about it," Aliyah said. "Field hockey is really not that complicated."

Fiona glanced at the booklet again and then shoved it into her bag. "I'm really not worried about the rules at all," she said.

"You're not?" Selma asked, confused.

Fiona shook her head. "I hate studying. I don't want to do it," she explained.

"It won't take long," Selma said. "Pretty soon you'll be a pro."

Fiona looked down. Then she said, "The truth is, I'm mostly worried about Jess and Paula making my life miserable."

Chapter 5

GOAL?

Fiona had all weekend to get to know the rules of field hockey. Her mom even found a cable channel that was showing a couple of field hockey games played by teams from Europe.

"They're showing a few games this weekend," her mom said. "It would be a fun way to learn the sport!"

But Fiona just shrugged. It still felt like studying to her.

So instead of studying the rules booklet or watching field hockey on TV that weekend, Fiona e-mailed with her friends back home. Then she set up an ice hockey goal in the back yard and practiced slapshots with her lucky puck.

"This counts as practice," she said to herself. "Staying in shape is staying in shape, right?"

By the time Monday came around, she didn't know any more about field hockey than she had all week. And after school, she had to go to field hockey practice.

"Okay, girls," Coach Kelly said once the team had gathered around her on the field. "First of all, congratulations to all of you for making the team. We had a big turnout this year, so you should be proud."

"Some of us prouder than others," Jess said with smirk.

Paula laughed. She looked right at Fiona and added, "Or luckier."

"Today, before we get into drills, we'll do a short scrimmage," the coach went on. Then she divided up the girls into two teams.

This time, Fiona ended up on a team with Jess and Paula.

"Great," Paula said after the teams were picked. "We have the hockey hick on our team."

Jess laughed like that was the funniest thing she'd ever heard. "Hockey hick," she repeated. "That's hilarious, Paula."

"Ha ha," Fiona said without smiling. "Why don't you two leave me alone?"

Jess stepped right up to her. "Why don't you go back to the farm?" she said.

Fiona narrowed her eyes. She decided she'd better show them how good she was at hockey. That was the only way they'd stop teasing her.

As soon as play started, Fiona got the ball and started driving up the field. Even though Selma and Aliyah were on the other team, she could tell that they were rooting for her.

"Nice one, Fiona," Selma called out. "Bring it all the way down."

Fiona didn't need to bring it all the way down, though. The goalie didn't look ready. *I've got this one,* she thought. So Fiona drew back and slapped the ball straight into the goal.

Everyone on the field stopped and looked at her. All the girls made faces like Fiona was insane. Even the coach seemed stunned.

Must have been a pretty great shot, Fiona thought. *They're all speechless.*

Then suddenly, Fiona heard laughter. Jess and Paula's laughter, of course.

"Um, hick," Jess said. "What was that?"

Fiona felt her face go red as she started to reply. "Um, a goal?" she said.

Jess and Paula nearly fell over laughing. That's when Fiona felt a hand on her shoulder.

"Take a seat on the bench, Fiona," the coach said sternly. "We'll talk after practice."

Fiona was confused as she dropped onto the bench. She had scored a great goal, hadn't she?

Fiona looked at the field at Selma and Aliyah. Both of them just looked back and shook their heads.

Chapter 6

CUT?

After practice, Coach Kelly told Fiona to change and come to her office. Fiona hurried to change back into her school clothes. Then she knocked on the coach's office door.

"Come in, Fiona," Coach Kelly said. She was sitting at her big desk in her office.

Fiona sat across from the coach in a rickety plastic chair. She nervously cleared her throat.

"You haven't studied the rules, have you?" the coach asked.

"Um, a little," Fiona replied.

"Very little, I'd guess," Coach Kelly said. "Do you know why that wasn't a goal today?"

"Was I off-sides?" Fiona asked. She didn't think she had been past all the defenders when she shot, but it was possible that she'd missed someone.

"There are no off-sides in field hockey," Coach Kelly replied. "Which just proves that you haven't studied."

"Oh," Fiona said quietly.

The coach sighed loudly. "The goal didn't count because to shoot you must be inside the striking circle," the coach said.

"The . . . striking circle?" Fiona repeated.

The coach sighed again. "You'd probably think of it as the crease," the coach explained. "That's the ice hockey term for it."

Fiona smiled and nodded. "Oh," she said. "Gotcha. You have to be inside the crease — I mean, the striking circle — to score a goal."

Coach Kelly shook her head slowly. "I took a chance putting you on the team, Fiona," the coach said. "You're new here, and you love ice hockey. You're obviously a good athlete. But you haven't kept up your part of the bargain."

Fiona looked down at the ground. Then she quietly asked, "Are you cutting me from the team?"

"No. Not yet," Coach Kelly replied. "You'll sit the bench this week and watch. On Friday, you'll practice with the team again. But if by the end of this week you don't have a better grasp of the rules, I'm going to have to cut you."

Chapter 7

CRAMMING

"I can't believe this," Fiona mumbled. She was leaning her chin on her fist. With her other hand, she used a fork to poke at her lunch.

"I know," Selma said. She stirred the slop in her bowl. "I can't believe this is actually beef stew either."

Aliyah nodded. "It's definitely not beef. Probably rat," she said. She gave her bowl a poke. "Or maybe stray cat."

"Gross," Fiona said, shaking her head to get rid of the image. "Anyway, I mean I can't believe I'm going to get cut from a hockey team!"

Aliyah waved her off. "You're not going to get cut," she said.

"But Coach Kelly said . . . ," Fiona started.

"Don't worry about that," Selma cut in. "We'll make sure you know what you need to know."

Aliyah managed a small bite of her stew. It made her shudder. Then she said, "Right. Come over to my place after practice today and we'll study."

Fiona sighed. "I can't believe I have to study that dumb booklet or get cut from the team," she said.

"Forget the booklet," Aliyah replied. "Selma and I know the rules. Plus we have lots of great videos. And we can practice in the park near Selma's apartment."

Selma nodded. "Definitely," she said. "The soccer field will be a good place to practice."

* * *

For the rest of the week, whenever Fiona wasn't in class or doing her homework, she was with Selma and Aliyah, trying to learn all the rules of field hockey.

They watched hours of field hockey videos at Aliyah's house. Some of the videos were of the middle school's team from last season. Some of them were of great pro teams from all over the world. Fiona took notes and watched carefully.

They also spent hours running up and down the soccer field at the park. Fiona was finally getting used to that crazy candy-cane hockey stick.

By the end of the week, Fiona was feeling pretty ready for practice.

"This is the big day, Fiona," Selma said. The three girls were changed and heading to the field for practice.

"Yeah," Aliyah added. "Today Coach Kelly will decide if you get to stay on the team or not. How do you feel? Are you nervous?"

Fiona smiled. "I feel pretty good about it," she said. "Quiz me."

Selma thought for a second, and then asked, "How do we restart play after an injury?"

Fiona knew that one right away. "A bully," she replied. "I'll never forget that after last week."

"Are you allowed to touch the ball, ever, with any part of your body?" Aliyah asked.

"Nope," Fiona said. "Not even to knock it down."

"And what if you do touch the ball?" Selma asked quickly.

"It's a penalty, called advancing," Fiona replied. "I really know this stuff, thanks to you guys!"

"Sounds like it," Aliyah agreed. "Now let's show the coach."

Fiona nodded as the girls headed toward the field. She was ready.

Chapter 8

ONE MORE CHANCE

"New teams today," Coach Kelly announced. She divided up the girls for a scrimmage. This time, Fiona was on team A with Selma and Aliyah. Paula and Jess were on team B.

"Remember, our first real game is next week," the coach said. "So today's practice won't be drills and exercises. We'll just play as hard as we can, okay?"

"Yes, Coach," the girls all replied.

"Good," the coach said. "You have your teams. Selma, you're in goal for team A. And Paula, I want you in goal for your team."

With that, the coach blew her whistle. The two centers faced each other, and Coach Kelly dropped the ball between them. "Team A starts," Coach Kelly said.

Team A's center passed the ball to the left, where Aliyah took control of the ball and started running up the field. Fiona ran forward too, hoping for a chance to score a goal the right way.

"Hey, pass it to the hick!" Paula yelled from the goal. "Maybe she wants to take a shot from out of bounds!"

Aliyah sneered at Paula. But Jess, playing defense for team B, laughed.

"Fiona probably wants to take a shot from the cafeteria!" Jess taunted. Paula cracked up laughing.

I'll show you how I want to shoot, Fiona thought. She cut into the striking circle and waved at Aliyah.

"Here!" she called out.

Aliyah nodded and drew back her stick. It looked like she was going to shoot.

With a loud slap, the ball flew toward Fiona. Fiona watched the flying white ball closely, and then raised her stick. The ball struck her stick at an angle. Then it veered off, headed right at the goal.

Paula looked shocked. The ball had changed direction so quickly, she didn't have time to recover. In a split second, the ball was in the back of the net.

"Goal, team A," Coach Kelly called out. She blew her whistle. "Good job, Fiona," she said. "That was a smart play you just made."

"Thanks, Coach," Fiona said. She jogged back to midfield. For the first time since she'd moved to River City, she felt good.

Team B won the scrimmage, but to Fiona, that didn't matter much. She was more concerned about whether she'd get to stay on the team.

After practice, Coach Kelly told everyone to hit the showers and have a good weekend.

"Fiona," the coach added quickly. "Stay here and talk to me, please."

Fiona glanced at Aliyah and Selma, who both shrugged.

"Yes, Coach?" Fiona said nervously. She watched as the rest of the team headed to the locker room.

"Before you get cleaned up and changed, I wanted to have a quick chat," Coach Kelly said.

"Okay," Fiona said.

The coach sat on the bench on the sideline and patted the seat next to her. Fiona sat down. "Remember the talk we had on Monday after practice?" the coach asked.

Fiona nodded. "Of course I do," she said. "I've been studying a lot."

"Have you?" Coach Kelly asked.

"Yes!" Fiona insisted. "Selma and Aliyah have helped me a lot. We watched a bunch of videos and practiced in the park."

"That was very nice of them," Coach Kelly said.

"Yes, it was," Fiona agreed.

"Well," the coach said, "I have to say, I was impressed with your playing today."

"Thanks," Fiona said, smiling.

"I could have called a penalty or two on you," the coach added quickly. "You obstructed twice."

"I did?" Fiona said.

The coach nodded. "Everyone does sometimes," she added. "It's usually not worth calling. Just wastes time."

"I read about that," Fiona said. "The advantage rule."

"That's right," the coach said. "What is the advantage rule?"

Fiona quickly answered, "If the penalty doesn't cause an advantage for the team, it shouldn't be called unless it was a dangerous play."

"Very good," Coach Kelly said.

Fiona smiled. "So," she said slowly, "have you decided whether you're going to cut me or not?"

The coach looked at the ground and sighed. "Well," she said, "I have decided."

"And?" Fiona asked.

"And I am not going to cut you," the coach said.

Fiona jumped up from the bench and shouted, "Yes!" She felt a huge smile growing on her face. "You won't regret this, Coach," she said, smiling.

"Not only that," the coach added, getting up from the bench, "I'd like you to start at right wing for our first game on Tuesday. Think you can do that?"

"Of course I can!" Fiona replied. "Totally!"

The coach laughed. "Great," Coach Kelly said. "Now go get cleaned up, and have a good weekend."

Fiona sprinted to the girls' locker room. She was thrilled. She was more than thrilled. She was so happy that she was still on the team!

"I made it!" she cried as she ran up to Aliyah and Selma.

"We knew you would," Selma replied.

"We wouldn't have wasted our time otherwise," Aliyah joked.

The three girls hugged.

"So are you happy you switched from ice to field?" Aliyah asked.

Fiona nodded. "Sure," she said. "And I'm just as happy to have two new friends on the team with me."

ABOUT THE AUTHOR

Eric Stevens lives in St. Paul, Minnesota. He is studying to become a middle-school English teacher. Some of his favorite things include pizza, playing video games, watching cooking shows on TV, riding his bike, and trying new restaurants. Some of his least favorite things include olives and shoveling snow.

ABOUT THE ILLUSTRATOR

When Tuesday Mourning was a little girl, she knew she wanted to be an artist when she grew up. Now, she is an illustrator who lives in South Pasadena, CA. She especially loves illustrating books for kids and teenagers. When she isn't illustrating, Tuesday loves spending time with her husband, who is an actor, and their two sons.

GLOSSARY

advantage (ad-VAN-tij)—something that helps or is useful to someone

bargain (BAR-guhn)—agreement

chaos (KAY-oss)—total confusion

checking (CHEK-ing)—using your body or stick to move or block another player

complicated (KOM-pli-kay-tid)—something that is difficult to understand

equipment (i-KWIP-muhnt)—the tools needed for a particular purpose

hick (HIK)—an insulting way to describe a person from a small town

miserable (MIZ-ur-uh-buhl)—sad, unhappy

overheard (oh-vur-HURD)—heard what someone else was saying without them knowing

penalty (PEN-uhl-tee)—a punishment that a team or player suffers for breaking the rules

scrimmage (SKRIM-ij)—a game played for practice

MORE ABOUT ICE HOCKEY AND FIELD HOCKEY

Most people think the only difference between ice hockey and field hockey is that ice hockey is played in a skating rink, and field hockey is played on a field. But there are other differences, too. Here are some of them.

RULES

OFF-SIDES: In ice hockey, an offensive player can't be in the attacking zone when the puck isn't in the attacking zone. But in field hockey, there's no off-sides rule.

FACE-OFF: To resume play in ice hockey, the official drops the puck between the two teams' centers, who then slap at the puck with their sticks. But in field hockey, play resumes with something called a bully. The ball rests on the field between two players. The players slap their sticks together three times, then slap at the ball.

CHECKING: In ice hockey, players are allowed to check, or use their bodies or sticks to push another player out of the way. Field hockey does not allowing checking, whether with a stick or a player's body.

SCORING: In ice hockey, a player can score from anywhere on the ice. However, in field hockey, players must be inside the striking circle to score. The striking circle is a semi-circle around the goal.

EQUIPMENT

Field hockey players wear cleats, but ice hockey players wear skates.

An ice hockey stick is shaped like an L, but a field hockey stick is shaped like a J.

Field hockey is played using a ball, but ice hockey is played using a puck.

DISCUSSION QUESTIONS

1. Fiona is new to her school. What are some ways to make friends when moving to a new place? What can you do to be friendly to someone who is new at your school?

2. Jess and Paula aren't very nice to Fiona. What are some ways to stand up to a bully?

3. Ice hockey was popular at Fiona's old school, but isn't at her new school. What sports are popular at your school? Are there other sports that you've heard of that aren't played at your school?

WRITING PROMPTS

1. Write about a time when you had to learn something new, even though it was difficult. What did you learn? How did you learn it?

2. Fiona makes friends with two girls on the field hockey team. Write about a friend you've made through an activity, sport, or other experience outside of school.

3. Have you ever had to move? Write about your experience. If you haven't had to move, write about someone you know who moved.

SPORTS STORIES
FOR EVERY ATHLETE

BY JAKE MADDOX

READ THEM ALL!